Stormiy Daze's

Patricia D. Bowe

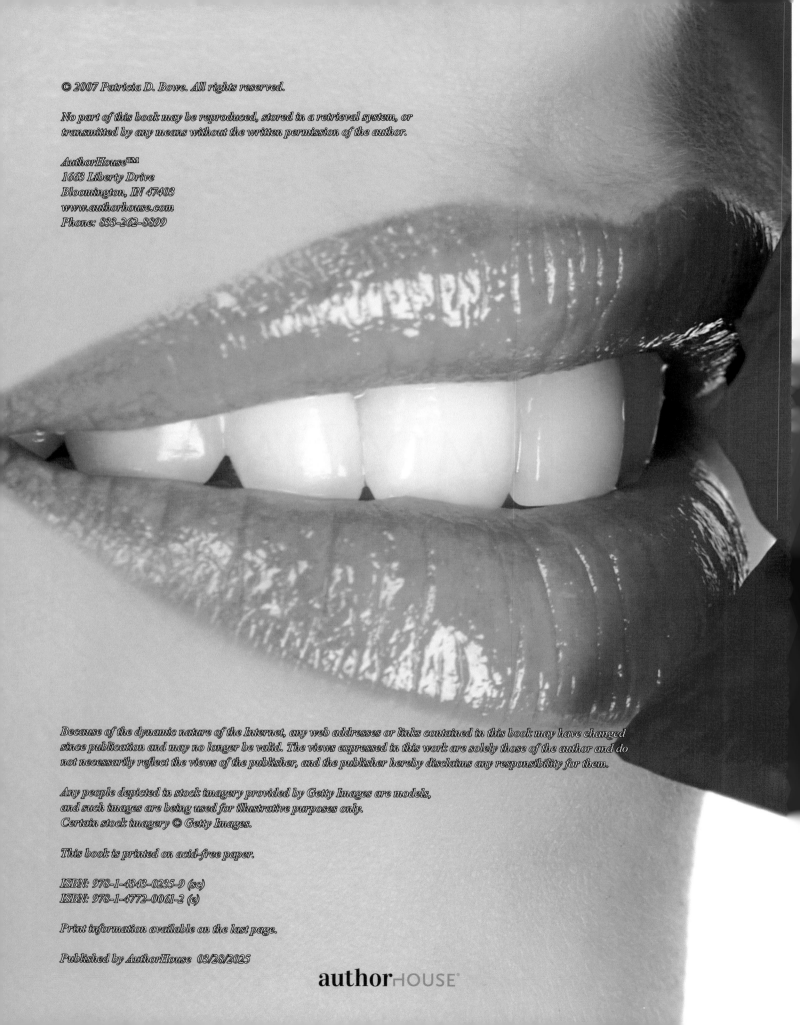

AuthorHouse™
1663 Liberty Drive
Bloomington, IN 47403
www.authorhouse.com
Phone: 833-262-8899

ISBN: 978-1-4343-0235-9 (sc)
ISBN: 978-1-4772-0061-2 (e)

Print information available on the last page.

Published by AuthorHouse 03/28/2025

authorHOUSE®

DEDICATION

1ST. & FOR MOST GOD THEN WITH LOVE TO MY SON'S CHRIS & DAVE FELTY & THERE FAMILY'S. MY EDITOR TODD D NELSON, & I DARE NOT FORGET MY AUNT ARNA MERRELL. LAST BUT NOT LEAST MY ALL TIME LOVE OF MY LIFE SCOTT MC COWAN GOD REST HIS SOUL!

ACKNOWLEGEMENT

1st. & for most God with him I can soar, My sons Chris & Dave Felty & there families for they are my heart & reason to always be a good person. With that hugs & kiss's. My wonderful Editor Todd D Nelson my better half for love & our long bull sessions on his day's off from his regular job. My Aunt Arna Merrell for her love & mercy as I was growing up for always knowing the right word's to say to me in time of trouble. Last but not least my all time love Scott MC Cowan,God rest his soul. He taught me what real love is, he is also the inspiration for several of my Poems 1: Into the moon lite 2: Where is she? And many more down the road that I will be writing. Of course I can't forget my dog Bogart & MY Teddy Bear too!

With much love Patricia D Bowe

CONTENTS

WHAT DO I SEE?

Look into my eyes what do you see? Tears, fear, sadness, happiness. Do you see the true me or do you see the me I want you to see. The 1 so tough no one can reach or touch. So strong, fearing if you could see the real me inside you would hate me. Does anyone see the real me, or have I hidden her so well behind my eyes. There are day's I don't even recognize the eyes in the mirror. Any more! until now you thought this was all about me but its not. Its about the tears I cry since you died. I used to see you in my eyes but now the only place I see you is in my heart. There are times your face doesn't come to me clearly & others days you in my own reflection.

TILL I MET YOU!!!

UNTIL I MET YOU, MY LIFE WAS FULL OF SADDNESS. UNTIL ECT ********** MY LIFE HAD NO MEANING. UNTIL ECT******* I WAS EMPTY AND I HAD NOWHERE, TO PUT MY TROUBLED HEART. UNTIL ECT ***** I HAD NO REASON TO SMILE.. TILL ECT*** I THOUGHT THERE WAS NO ONE TO LOVE ME OR THOUGHT THERE WAS NO ONE TO GIVE MY LOVE TOO. UNTIL ECT ******** I THOUGHT THERE WAS NO ONE I COULD SHARE MY WILDEST DREAMS OR PASSIONS WITH. TILL ECT ****** MY SOUL WAS FILLED WITH THE HORROR OF THE PAST, YET NOW MY SOUL IS FULL WITH JOY, TILL ECT***** I COULD'NT FLY , YET NOW I KNOW I CAN SOAR ABOVE THE CLOUDS SO BRIGHTLY AND DANCE THE DANCE OF A CHILD SET FREE FROM ALL HER FEARS. TO REACH FOR THAT ONE STAR THAT SEEMED IMPOSSIBLE TO REACH FOR. UNTIL ECT***** I DID NOT KNOW WHO I AM. ? NOW I KNOW I'M LOVED, I'M PASSIONATE, I'M BEAUTIFUL, I'M SEXY, ECT AND I HAVE A WONDERFUL GODLY MAN THAT LOVES ME AND ENCOUAGE ME TO GROW STRONG AND HEALTHY WITH HIM. UNTIL ECT ***** I HIDE MYSELF IN AN UNREACHABLE CAVE IN MY SOUL AND NOW I GREET EVER NEW DAY WITH THE FURY OF A WILD HORSE SET FREE FOR THE VERY FIRST TIME!!!! UNTIL ECT I BELIEVED ALL THE LIES AND HATEFUL WORDS AND NOW I KNOW I AM SPECIAL!!!!!! UNTIL ECT ******* THE FUTURE SEEMED IMPOSSIBLE AND NOW I AM ENBRACING IT, WITH THE JOY OF A NEW MAMA BIRD AS SHE LET HER BABY BIRD FLY FOR THE VERY 1'ST TIME. ! UNTIL I MET YOU. MY LOVE AND SOULMATE UNTIL !!!!!!!!!!!!!

FACES OR EYES

Everyday we pass so many people or others may call them strangers. Some you can almost feel there happiness, sadness Others scare you! As almost to look right though you! The innocence of children, the joy in there eyes. Their innocence has not yet been damaged by life's pain. The fear of the elderly, waiting to die, and those who wear a mask for whatever reason hiding in there very being. Their pain is so deep they can't escape it. I see a lady everday walking by my apartment, I say "hi" to her, she lowers her head with no response passing by so the world doesn't notice her. Makes me wonder if she's hiding fear, loneness or what? See looks so blank inside, almost catatonic. My heart and very soul goes out to her. For at one point in my life I was her. The kindness of others and doctors and friends got me though my despair. I just wish I could help this lady that walks by my place! Maybe some day! God will reach her!

PASSION

THIS WORD HAS SO MANY UNDERTONES,
MEANING ANYTHING FROM GREAT LOVE TO GREAT SORROW.
IT'S THE INNTER MOST BLIZFUL PART OF TWO SOULS
JOINING INTO ONE HEART, ONE BODY, AND ONE SOUL.
IN ADDITION, WHEN THE MIND IS PART OF THE WHOLE
    PICTURE, YOU HAVE FIREWORKS!!!!!!!!!!
BUSTING INTO THE SKY!!!!!!

I AM VERY PASSIONATE ABOUT:
MY LOVE FOR GOD, THE NEED TO HELP OTHERS,
NATURE'S PRESERVATION,
MY SENSUAL AND INTIMATE SIDES,
WRITING TO SHARE MY PAIN TO HELP OTHERS IN PAIN FROM THE PAST.

PASSION IS THE VERY ESSENCES OF TWO HEARTS JOIN INTO ONE
AS THEY MAKE LOVE TO EACH OTHER.
AS THEY EXPORE THE VERY BEING OF EACH OTHER'S ONENESS
TO CREATE ONE HEART BEAT, BETWEEN TWO SOULS.
TO INNTER LOCK WITH THE PASSION AND FIRE
THAT CLOSES THE REST OF THE WORLD OUT.

AND ONLY YOU AND I HEAR THE MUSIC
OF 1000 ANGLES CHEERING US ON WITH JOY.
FOR WE HAVE BECOME TOTALLY LOST
IN EACH OTHER'S VERY BEING.
WE SHARE ONE HEARTBEAT, ONE
   SOUL, AND ONE MIND.
OUR BODIES ARE IN TANGLED AS ONE
WITH OUR DESIRE FOR EACH OTHER.
THE DEPTHS OF THIS PASSION
   COULD LAST A LIFE TIME.
OR COULD BURN OUT FROM BETRAYAL.

THAT IS WHERE THE SORROW COMES
   INTO PLAY, FROM PASSION.
IT CAN CREATE MAGIC OR CREATE GREAT SORROW.

SO MY FRIEND BE CAREFUL TO WHOM YOU
   TRUST YOU PASSION WITH, BECAUSE IT
   CAN MAKE OR BREAK OUR VERY SOULS.
AS WELL AS TURN OUR WORLDS UPSIDE-DOWN!!!!!

I AM WILLING TO PUT MY PASSION IN YOUR ARMS.
   WILL YOU DO THE SAME???

IF I COULD FLY

<u>IF I COULD FLY!!!!!</u>
BE LIKE A BIRD HIGH IN THE SKY
FEEL THE WIND ALL AROUND
ME. SEE FOR MILES ABOVE THE
LAND. FEEL SO FREE AS I'M ONE
WITH THE CLOUDS HIGHER AND
HIGHER AS I FLY IN AND OUT OF
THEM. SEARING FOR THE ANWERS
TO ALL MY DREAMS. KNOWING
I AM TRULY FREE TO SOAR INTO
THE HEAVENS IN SEARCH OF MY
FOREVER. ONLY IF I COULD FLY????

INTO THE MOONLITE

INTO THE MOONLITE, I LOOK WITH AMAZEMENT!!!! I WONDER
IF IT'S REALLY US? DANCING WITH SUCH A FREEDOM AROUND
THIS SNOWEY WHITE CLOUD, IN AND OUT OF THE SPARKING
STARS; OR IS IT A DREAM COME TRUE? FILLED WITH MAGIC AND
WONDERMENT AS YOU HOLD ME EVER SO CLOSE TO YOU. I CAN
HARDLY TAKE A BREATH. WE ARE DANCING AS IF WE ARE LOST
IN EACH OTHERS SOULS. WE HAVE TRULY FOUND THAT ONENESS
WHICH NO ONE BUT US UNDERSTAND. NO ONE CAN REACH US
WHEN WE ARE IN THIS STATE OF PASSION AND ONENESS. I AM
LOST IN YOUR SOUL, AS YOU ARE LOST IN MINE!!!! I KNOW WE
WANT DIFFERENT THINGS IN OUR FUTURE BUT TRULY, WE WANT
THE SAME THINGS. WE JUST DO NOT WANT ANYONE TO TAKE OUR
DREAM AWAY! SO LET US JOIN FORCES AND SUPPORT EACHOTHER
IN DREAMS AND BUILD EACHOTHER UP!!!!! NOT TAKE A WAY FROM
EACH OTHER BUT ENCOUAGE AND GROW TOGETHER AS ONE!!!!
FOR YES, I CAN DANCE ALONE INTO THE MOONLITE, BUT ITS
MORE FULFILLING WHEN I DANCE WITH YOU IF ONLY INTO THE
MOONLITE, WILL MY DREAM START TO BLOSSOM INTO THE REAL
THING HIDDEN IN MY HEART AND VERY SOUL. I PRAY YOU WILL BE
THERE WITH ME. IF ONLY TO DANCE INTO THE MOONLITE, WE WILL
MEET!!!!!! I WILL BE THERE! WILL YOU?!!!!!!!

LOVE

Oh love it can be so wonderful or oh so painful. But most of all love should be unconditional. Not the games of you give me this and I'll take that. So on and on. You can't put a price on love or force anyone to love you. It's not a game to use to get sex. Love is the most wonderful gift God has given us to give each other. Love can devastate. So never take it lightly, but cherish it, because love can be gone in a heartbeat.

SEASONS CHANGE

MUST, ALL EXPERIENCES EVOLVE AND HAVE
AN ENDING EVEN FREINDSHIPS? MAKES
ONE WONDER WHY SOME LAST THE TEST OF
TIME INTO THE GREAT BEYOND AND OTHERS
END LIKE A CHAPTER IN A BOOK... END
THEY ARE ONLY THERE FOR A SHORT TIME TOO GET
US THROUGH SOME GREAT BEGINNING OF PASSAGE
IN LIFE'S JOURNEY AND END AS ABRUPTLY. ALWAYS
PAINFUL, YET FILLED WITH THE SAME ENERGY OF
THAT PASSION THAT STARTED THE WHOLE THING IN
THE FIRST PLACE. SOMETIMES WE FIGHT CHANGE,
BECAUSE I BELEIVE WE, AS HUMANS, ARE HORRIFIED
OF THE UNKNOWN. HOWEVER, ALL LIFE'S CHANGES
ARE NOT FOR THE WORST, BUT ARE FOR OUR BEST.
FOR US TO LEARN AND GROW AND BECOME WHO GOD
INTENDS FOR US TO BE IN THAT MOMENT, WE GIVE
 TO EACH OTHER MAKING
 THAT JOURNEY AN EASIER PATH TO TRAVEL.
 YET, I AM NOT SAYING IT DOESN'T
COME WITHOUT PAIN
 FOR IN PAIN WE TRULY LEARN THE
MEANING AND VAULE OF LIFES MIRACE

WHERE IS SHE?

She's not here nor there. She's got to be somewhere!
Wow! She's lost in the confusion of her life. In the
shaking of her own hands. She feels lost and hopeless,
but most of all, scared of what you may say or think
of her. People just don't know what it is like for her
now. With the Superwoman act on the outside, no one
has seen here pain until now. That it's overflowing
and pouring out as she yelling for help. I guess even
Superheroes need help sometimes. I truly can't believe
she's come through so much and how deeply it has
devastated her. So as she still watch's her hands shake,
I'm here to say she is grateful to God and others for
grace and mercy shown to here in her time of need.
From a few , the kind words, the trying to make her
laugh bunch. The young girls who call her mom or
friend. To all she says Thank you for being there for
her and most of all Thanks to God for all the love and
compassion she was shown. The hugs were there for her
too. So where is she?She's in all of YOU! She's left the
super stuff to someone else for a while.Because right
now, she's the one who needs the super help. (Sigh.)

TEDDY BEAR VS. PEOPLE

Why I prefer teddy bears to people, they don't talk back ,judge you, beat you down, swear, & so on .People will beat you down till there is nothing better to do then run to your favorite teddy bear in panic you pick it up then start telling it about your bad day until you sob yourself to sleep. So next time you pass a toy store pick up a few teddy bears for a friend or two they last longer then any friendship I've ever had & last longer then flowers too! Wow I better run to the toy store and get a couple more teddy bears ha ha --------------ha. All joking a side not all people are bad but I still prefer my teddy bear after all who else can you tell a secret too, and know it will be save forever.! Uh? Thing about it!

NITEMARES & NITETERRORS

I lay here in my bed wondering what terror I will have to battle tonight. Who will or what will I see? knowing I must sleep or I won't be able to cope the next day… OH No! here they come the monsters the memories of the past hurts past abuse here they start all over again. You get to where you fear sleep for the battle will start as it did like the night before. Screaming & shaking you wake, trying to remember what terrorized you, Falling asleep again only to leave off where you started in this terror you feel as if you can't breath your yelling in a panic but no one can hears you. With no avail you can't awaken this nitemare hell night after night. Somebody help me! God help me! Years of therapy won't even stop the demons of the night What's a person to do? What I have learned, yes the nite terrors may still be coming, They are just that terrors & there not real. Yes terrors will scare you but thank God the terrors can't really hurt us. OF course It will take time to realize it. So sleep tight my friend, hope I see you save in dream land!

ROSES HAVE THORNS

When she was a little girl, will name her Misty for name sack. She believed the world was beautiful. She was young, naïve didn't have a care in the world. Mistiy'S Grandma would always tell her some day you will realize Roses have Thorns. She would go though her ever day life with out a care in the world, yet in the back of her mind those words would be ringing Roses have thorns. To her dismay she would try to dismiss it with no avail, Those words were always there. After all roses are beautiful, aromatic, soft, until she clutched it up firmly from the ground as her hand flowed she screamed! I now get it. Even the most frails of circumstance can hurt you! Mistiy stated to take those words to heart ,way up into HER adulthood. Ever good situation had a painful lesson to it. Now it was clutching at her heart & Not at her fingers as years before! Look out for those thorns!!! JUST Remember ROSES HAVE THORNS!!!

SAFE PLACE IN MY MIND

She has a special hiding place in her mind, to run away
from abuse. It's a calm place at the beach where she can
wash a way the stress of her days. The sky is blue the water
is cool as night slowly rolls in, She has a better perspective
of her worried day. AS she walks along the beach she feels
the sand in between her toes. Not a care now of her tragic
life, for she is truly safe now & will be forever, now, As
she realizes she can never turn back she must take control
of her own safety now, She can be strong & leave! & walk
forward with her life head held high, she feel's the first
smile on her face in year. She can move forward will You?!

LIGHT HEARTED LION

I once knew an arrogant, egotistical, pretentious, so on & so. Oh man I tell you ,
he drove me insane just to much. They can't put out all there feels like us women
do cause they are scared of being laugh at or cry baby as such that. So the be
these overbearing apes so not to look human or something. I think there all big
light hearted lions push over babies .after all who for nine month pack that baby
around now really! Think about it!!! That's why men are light hearted lions.
Roarrrrrrrrrrrrrrrrrrrrrrrrrrrrrrrrrrrrrrrrrrrrr ha ha!

DOG DAZE'S

Bogart is his name, I found him at the local pound, he was all scare in the
back of his cage I called to him, he came shaking to the front of the cage
I touched his head & that was that we belonged to each other from that day on.
He is a real cool pup loving, loyal, and tell you protective too. My
neighbor's think he's a nut case see he do this silly spring board thing,
jump jump IT nuts. Like most pets he's not a pet he's family. He's great
company for my better half & I. Have you hugged you pet today?

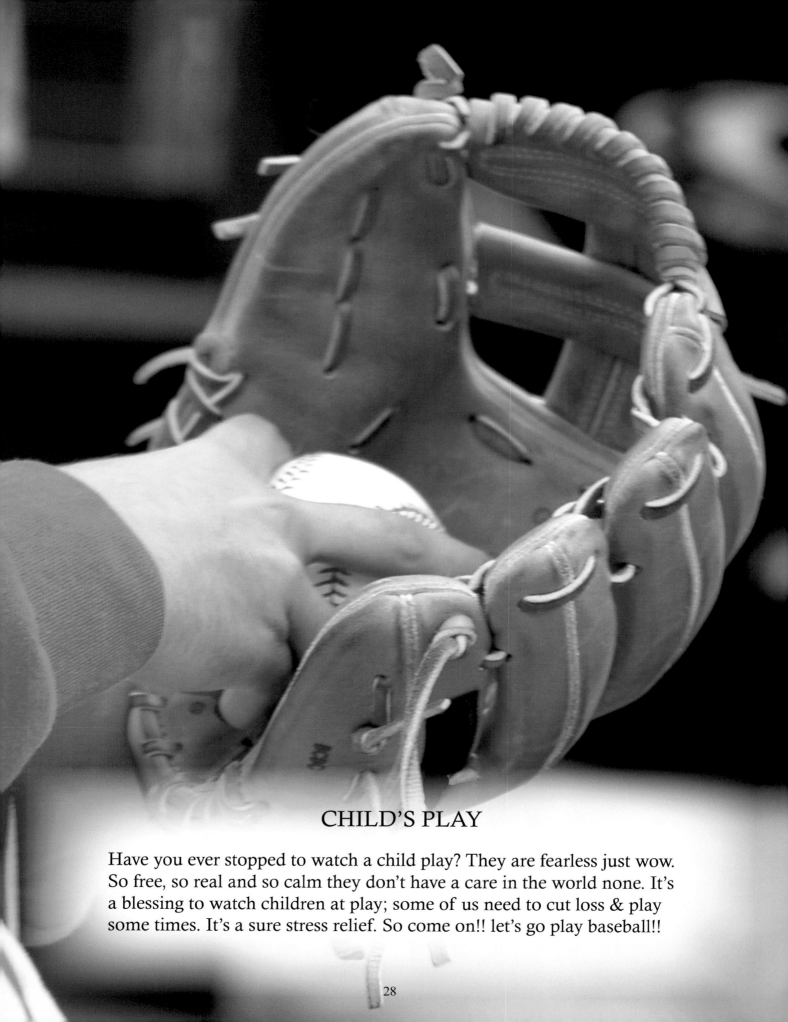

CHILD'S PLAY

Have you ever stopped to watch a child play? They are fearless just wow.
So free, so real and so calm they don't have a care in the world none. It's
a blessing to watch children at play; some of us need to cut loss & play
some times. It's a sure stress relief. So come on!! let's go play baseball!!

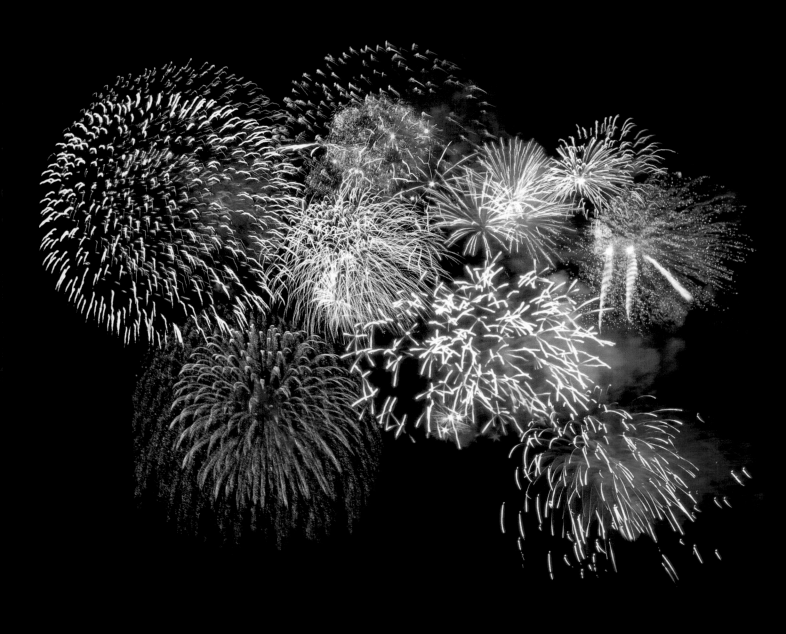

SPLENDOR IN THE SKYS

Boom, Bang &color in its splendor in the glorious sky. A person yelling with excitement over the array of color hit's the skys in its marvel. The celebration!! As the, exploding fireworks hit the skys

SNUGGLE TIME

Oh this is nice all warm & cozy yes I like this, as
the little cub all cuddle together ONE cub say's
where mom? I am hungry. Mom oh mom!!!

ROCKS ARE MORE THAN STONES

There nice for fish bowls, gardens, luck, worry & lets not forget the pet rock too…. I have a many worry & good luck stones. Different culture's value the rock as sacred for one reason or an other. They also can be polished, cut, &be turned into beautiful gems I Love the colored stone ones that are used for luck & so on. After all remember diamond come from a stone!!!!!

SUMMER OF LOVE

It was the summer of my college graduation. Love was in the air, I only had two month left until my Wedding. Now I can focus on getting ready, there were still dress fittings, place setting to pick out, flowers to order and a bacheloret party too. MY heart was just pounding with joy. Steve & I had been engaged since high school, after five years of school we were still madly in love as we were at our engage Party. Soon it would be the big day, To be Husband & Wife our Wedding celebration will be at the beach in Mississippi where we meet at Jr. College, our eye first meet & it was love at first sight. Steve loved my blonde locks & I loved his marvelous smile. I am so proud to be Steve's bride & partner. Well Dear Journal it's time for me to get some sleep, another day has passed sigh Stormiy

Patricia D Bowe (Stormiy) is retired in her
middle 50s. I live in southren calif. I'm like alot
of young girls of the 60's childhold was a life of
surviveing the abuse. Which I have learned alot. I
tell you my book is to help those that understand
my pain male or female. I am very happy now
still scared at times. I have PTSD/ Bipoalor.
MY grown sons 2 of them live in Idaho with my
grandkids. Thats why plus God I am sane today.
MY family is my heart!!!!! Writteng this book is
my passion & soul.

Printed in the United States
by Baker & Taylor Publisher Services